THE GUARDIAN'S VIGIL

A SHORT STORY

ALEXANDRIA BLAELOCK

BlueMere Books
MELBOURNE, AUSTRALIA

Publisher's Note: This is a work of fiction. Names, characters, places, and incidents are a product of the author's imagination. Locations and public names are sometimes used for atmospheric purposes. Any resemblance to actual people, living or dead, or to businesses, companies, events, institutions, or locations is completely coincidental.

Copyright © 2020 Alexandria Blaelock.

All rights reserved. No part of this publication may be reproduced, distributed or transmitted in any form or by any means, including photocopying, recording, or other electronic or mechanical methods, without the prior written permission of the publisher, except in the case of brief quotations embodied in critical reviews and certain other non-commercial uses permitted by copyright law.

For permission requests, please contact enquiries@bluemerebooks.com.

Ordering Information:
Discounts are available on quantity purchases. For details, contact orders@bluemerebooks.com.

The Guardian's Vigil/Alexandria Blaelock
paperback ISBN: 978-1-925749-26-7
digital ISBN: 978-1-925749-27-4

Book Layout © BookDesignTemplates.com

BlueMere Books
www.bluemerebooks.com

THE GUARDIAN'S VIGIL

Elspeth stood on the headland, poised as if to leap. Her gaze scudded up and down the horizon.

Her mind and body were almost paralysed by foreboding, as fisher wives often are.

The coarse fabric of her plaid skirt eddied around her legs in the stiff breeze as if trying to devour them.

The purple primroses surrounding her bowed and bobbed their heads as they danced a reel and gossipped amongst themselves.

She tried to remember a time when she hadn't been standing, watching and waiting, but it felt like she'd been there forever.

Like a tree, her roots diving deep into the cliffs and branches looking in all directions. She shifted restlessly, unwilling to look away.

Trapped, unable to escape.

And she was tired, so very tired.

Not even the deafening noise of the Puffins nesting in the cliff was enough to keep her alert.

The waves crashing on the shore were hypnotic, and she found herself eyes closed, swaying backwards and forwards with the rhythm.

She forced herself to still and squinted again out into the ocean.

Not for the first time, she cursed the circumstances that brought her to the headland.

The phantom aromas of her childhood enveloped her; the dark, brooding blue ocean, the elusive sweetness of the primrose, and the pale, dry scent of wood stacked behind her.

Times were good then.

Plentiful harvests producing more than enough food for everyone.

Singing, dancing and making merry on feast days.

Even the daily chores were infused with fun and laughter.

She saw herself young and carefree, chasing birds, and stray black-faced sheep.

Times the like of which she'd never see again.

She peered over the cliffs, into the heaving ocean.

It would be so easy to escape her obligation, but she'd chosen the dangerous path, and there was no turning back now.

Ghostly clouds passed over the moon, and a smattering of raindrops fell.

Elspeth tugged her shawl more tightly around her, shivered, and bent into the wind.

THE GUARDIAN'S VIGIL

She was waiting, always waiting.

If only the waiting were over.

One way or another.

A light mist lifted from the ocean and caressed her in passing. As if the ghosts of her ancestors were all about her, gnashing their teeth.

She frowned, unable to see clearly.

"Look at what you've done," the ghosts seemed to say, "you can never fix a broken pot."

She strained her ears for sounds in the distance, but all was silent.

Soon, any time now.

The loneliness was the hardest to bear.

She craved the company of someone to share the vigil. A human heart beating in time with hers, reassuring her that she was not alone.

That it wasn't in vain.

It was forbidden anyway; this was *her* vigil.

Too many dead to do it in pairs anyway.

She almost wished she'd been taken by the faeries. At least she'd be having a merry, and well-fed time.

The end result would be the same.

If Elspeth went back, the village would be gone, as if it had never been there.

They'd spared a few scraps to sustain her for the vigil.

After that, she'd be on her own.

Slowly she chewed and ate a dry crust of bread, never once looking away from the heaving ocean.

She knew other Guardians were in their places, keeping their own vigils.

She looked up and down the coast for the prearranged signals, but none were to be seen.

It was easy to believe they were all gone, no one left but her.

Her feet took her a few steps closer to the nearest before she recalled her duty.

At least her bairns would be safe, though she wished she could see them one more time, and hold their little bodies close to hers.

They'd grow old without her.

She wouldn't arrange their marriages or assist at the births of her grandchildren.

But they'd survive. Though she couldn't help but worry about them.

If only there were some way to know that her sacrifice wouldn't be in vain.

Memories surged around her as she thought of her husband; tall and strong with a ready smile and a beautiful singing voice.

He was a gentle and caring man, a good provider and a good husband who never beat her. But he was a man made for peacetime, unable to cope with the times that had come upon them.

The wailing of hunger left him as desolate as the fallow fields.

The animals were gone, and even the fish wouldn't come to the nets.

They'd been happy once, blessed with three beautiful and obedient children.

Maybe they were blessed by the gods, perhaps in payment for what was to come.

He wasn't a man fit for war, as unsuited to it as a fish is to dry land.

She'd wished more than once in her life she'd been born with the power. A witch's life may be hard and lonely, but at least she wouldn't be cold or hungry.

And she'd have been in the village with all that she held dear.

The pipes wailed as she listened with her heart, and wondered where the happy times had gone. The times of joy and love, when all the world was secure.

When no one feared the rising of the new day or the waning of the old.

She wished there'd been a moment to say goodbye.

But once the decision was made, she and the other Guardians were out of the village almost before they knew what'd happened.

Perhaps her friends and family didn't even know what she was doing. Maybe they thought she was so scared she had run away, as others had.

Cursed!

They were all cursed. The healer had the right of it, but he'd been taken before he could give them the guidance they had so desperately needed.

The gods had not seen fit to give them a new guide.

The men had taken a council and had made up their own minds over what was to be done. The village must be protected above all else.

They were truly forsaken.

Her vigil was wasted, and the evil would come upon them unprepared. The sky wept fitfully along with her.

She wondered why she'd chosen to do this thing. She'd never see her precious bairns, or friends again.

How could she survive without them?

She tasted the agony of it, bitter in the back of her throat.

Nameless dread pumping around her body in her blood.

She firmly swallowed it all down with the bread and forced her eyes back to the horizon.

At last, she saw what she'd been searching for, this night and many more.

THE GUARDIAN'S VIGIL

Unable to believe her eyes, she rubbed at them and looked again.

The sails were still there.

Straining her ears, she could hear the creak of the Viking boats.

She pinched herself, it was not a dream.

She fumbled in her pocket for her flint, her fingers almost numb with the cold.

She struck it again, and again, her tremors nearly overcoming her before the dry tinder caught.

The tiny flames grew, and the wood started to burn.

She danced a little around the fire, urging the flames to grow, and slowly they did.

Then she threw herself to the ground and wept.

It was all over.

It was going to be all right.

The beacon was lit, and the village would be prepared.

She saw the other fires light up and down the coast one by one, like a string of garnets sparkling in candlelight.

Then she felt the tingling in her body and smelled the green acidic, oily scent which could only mean the witch had begun her spells.

Only then did she shut her eyes, and end her ceaseless vigilance.

The village was protected.
The gods could do with her whatever they willed, her task, and her life was over.

THE END

ABOUT THE AUTHOR

Alexandria Blaelock writes stories, some of them for *Ellery Queen's Mystery Magazine* and *Pulphouse Fiction Magazine*. She's also written four self-help books applying business techniques to personal matters like getting dressed, cleaning house, and feeding your friends.

As a recovering Project Manager, she's probably too fond of sticking to plan. She lives in a forest because she enjoys birdsong, the scent of gum leaves and the sun on her face. When not telecommuting to parallel universes from her Melbourne based imagination, she watches K-dramas, talks to animals, and drinks Campari. At the same time.

Discover more at www.alexandriablaelock.com.

OTHER SHORT STORIES BY ALEXANDRIA BLAELOCK

Kiss of Death
Long Weekend in the Snow
Shining Star
Phoenix Child
Ship in a Bottle
Lady of the Looking Glass
Simone Says Hands in the Air
Life in the Security Directorate
Fate in Your Hands
Love in the Security Directorate
Alma's Grace
Payton's Run
The Guardian's Vigil
The Life and Death of Carmelita Basingstoke
Balancing the Book

BOOKS BY ALEXANDRIA BLAELOCK

Stress Free Dinner Parties
Build Your Signature Wardrobe
Holistic Personal Finance
Ms Blaelock's Book of Minimally Viable Housekeeping

Lightning Source UK Ltd.
Milton Keynes UK
UKHW021023210820
368606UK00016B/1107